Nate the Great
Goes Down in the Dumps

Nate the Great

Goes Down in the Dumps

by Marjorie Weinman Sharmat
illustrated by Marc Simont

A Yearling Book

Published by
Yearling
an imprint of
Random House Children's Books
a division of Random House, Inc.
New York

Visit us on the Web! www.randomhouse.com/kids

Educators and librarians, for a variety of teaching tools, visit us at www.randomhouse.com/teachers

ISBN: 0-440-40438-X

Reprinted by arrangement with The Putnam Publishing Group Inc.

Printed in the United States of America

One Previous Edition

New Yearling Edition January 2006

40 39 38 37 36 35 34 33 32

UPR

For my dog, Fritz Melvin,

who came into my life

when Sludge came into Nate's

—M.W.S.

I, Nate the Great,

and my dog, Sludge,

were taking a walk.

We walked too far.

We walked to Rosamond's house.

Rosamond and her four cats were

sitting on a crate

behind a table

in front of her house.

There was a crystal ball
on the table.
There was a sign
next to the crystal ball.

"I will read your future,"
Rosamond said. "For two cents."
"My future is worth more
than two cents," I said.
"Three cents, then," Rosamond said.

She gazed into her crystal ball.

"You will have a new case to solve very soon. Three cents."

"I, Nate the Great, always have cases to solve," I said.

Rosamond gazed into her crystal ball again.

"I can tell you more," she said.

"Someone has lost a box, a money box. You have to look for it."

"A money box?" I said.

"How much money is in it?"

"No money," Rosamond said.

"It's empty."

"Empty?"

"Yes. It's my box.

I was going to use it
to hold the money I got
for reading the future."
Sludge was tugging at me to leave.
He did not see any money
in Rosamond's future.
"Don't go," Rosamond said.
"Listen to what happened.
Claude helped me set up my business.
We brought out the table,
this sign, the box,
and four cans of tuna fish
for my cats.
Cats want to know
what's in their future, too.
Like tuna fish."

"Of course," I said.

"I put the sign on the table,"
Rosamond said.

"I put the box on the grass
near the table.

I put the tuna-fish cans
in a neat pile near the box."

"What happened next?" I asked.

"My cats and I went into my house

to get my crystal ball," Rosamond said.

"Claude went into my garage

to get this crate

for my cats and me to sit on.

When I came back with my crystal ball

the crate was here.

The table and the sign

and the tuna-fish cans were still here.

But the cans were tipped over.

The box and Claude were gone."

"When did this happen?" I asked.

"Just before you came along,"
Rosamond said.

"You are my first customer
for reading the future.
Now you have a new case and
you owe me three cents."

"I don't have three cents," I said,
"and you don't have a box
to put it in."

"I will if you solve the case,"
Rosamond said.
"This is a very famous box.
It's the first box that my cat
Super Hex ever slept in."
Rosamond gave me a strange look.

It was the only kind of look she had.

"Very well," I said. "I will take your case.

Does your famous box have a cover?

Does it have a color? What size is it?"

"It's a white box with ROSAMOND

printed on one side of it," Rosamond said.

"It doesn't have a cover.

It's big enough to hold

one hundred dollars in pennies."

"How big is that?" I asked.

Rosamond pointed to her house.

"The box is smaller than my house,

smaller than my garage,

smaller than this crate,

smaller than—"

"Never mind," I said.

Rosamond shrugged. "I read the future.

I don't measure boxes."

I took out my notebook

and tore off a piece of paper.

I wrote a note to my mother.

Rosamond grabbed my note.

"I will deliver this

while you solve my case."

Rosamond walked off

with her four cats.

Sludge and I sat down on the crate.

Dear Mother,
I am on a case
you wouldn't
believe so I won't
tell you about it
I will be back.
Love
Nate the Great

The crate had a label on it: BANANAS.

"Maybe the box is still here

somewhere," I said.

Sludge and I peered under the table.

The box wasn't there.

Suddenly we saw legs. Six legs.

Two belonged to Annie,

and four belonged to her dog, Fang.

"Can you read my future?" Annie asked.

"No, but I can read Fang's future.

I, Nate the Great, predict that

someday Fang is going to bite

Sludge and me. Today could be the day."

Sludge and I rushed off.

I called back to Annie.

"Have you seen an empty box

with Rosamond's name on it,

and big enough to hold

one hundred dollars in pennies?"

"No," Annie shouted.

"We have to look for Claude,"

I said to Sludge.

Looking for Claude

would be harder

than looking for the box.

Claude was always getting lost.

We went to Claude's house.

I rang his doorbell.

I knocked on his door.

I peeked through his windows.

Somebody tapped me on the shoulder.

It was Claude.

"Are you looking for me?" he asked.

"I was lost but I found myself."

"Good work," I said.

"I am looking for Rosamond's box.

I think you saw it last."

"I saw it on the grass

just before I went into her garage

to get her crate," Claude said.

"Carrying that crate was hard work!

It kept bumping into my stomach.

I put it down on the grass by the table,

just where Rosamond wanted it.

All the time I kept watching

for Rosamond.

I hoped she wouldn't

come out before

I could get away."

"Get away?"

"Yes. I was tired of

being Rosamond's moving man.

After I put the crate down,

I started to run."

"Then what?"

"I tripped over the pile

of tuna-fish cans," Claude said.

"I fell down on the grass.

But the box wasn't there.

I would have seen it."

"That explains why the pile of cans

was tipped over," I said. "But

it doesn't explain where the box went.

I, Nate the Great, say that
somebody must have taken it
while you were in the garage
and Rosamond and her cats
were in her house.
But who would want an empty box
with Rosamond's name on it?"
Claude shrugged.
"Somebody extremely desperate
for a box," I said.
Sludge and I rushed to Finley's house.
Finley owns a rat. The rat sleeps
in a big box until he chews it up.
Then Finley gets a new box.
Maybe it was time for a new box
for Finley's rat.

Maybe Finley took Rosamond's box.
I saw Finley outside with his rat.
There was a big chewed-up box
beside the rat with RAT HOUSE
printed on it.

"I am looking for an empty box
big enough to hold
one hundred dollars in pennies,"
I said. "It belongs to Rosamond."
"My box belongs to my rat," Finley said.
"But there are plenty of boxes at the
supermarket. They have the best ones.
If you can't find Rosamond's box there,
go to the dump.
They have the worst ones."
"I will look for the best," I said.
"I, Nate the Great, do not like dumps."
Sludge and I went to the supermarket.
Sludge had to wait outside.
I went inside. I looked for empty boxes.
I saw open boxes and sacks

full of oranges and potatoes.

I saw open crates

full of tomatoes and bananas and carrots.

I saw labels on the boxes and crates.

I remembered that Rosamond's crate
had the label BANANAS on it.
She probably got her crate
at this supermarket.
But that was no help.
I, Nate the Great, did not need
a crate that said BANANAS
or a box that said ORANGES.
I needed a box that said ROSAMOND.
Suddenly I smelled something.
Pancakes.
A lady was handing out pancake samples.
I took one.
Then I circled around and took another.
The third time around she said,
"No more."

I left the supermarket.

I, Nate the Great, needed more
pancakes.

Sludge needed a bone.

We went home.

We ate and thought.

I kept thinking about the empty box.

There was something else empty, too.

My head.

Was I missing a big clue?

I thought back.

An empty box. A table. A sign.

Four cans of tuna fish.

Rosamond saw all these things

before she and her cats went

into her house.

Claude saw them before he went

into Rosamond's garage.

Then the empty box was gone.

Only the empty box.

Why?

Perhaps the table was too heavy

to take. And no one would take

a sign that said

ROSAMOND READS THE FUTURE. 2¢.

But why not take the cans of tuna fish?

Why take an empty box

that isn't worth anything?

I, Nate the Great, suddenly

had the answer!

Because the box isn't worth anything!

Someone must have seen the empty box

and picked it up and thrown it away.

But it had Rosamond's name on it.

Just on one side.

Maybe her name wasn't seen.

"Rosamond's box has probably gone

to the dump by now," I said to Sludge.

"Where the worst boxes go."

Sludge and I hurried to the town dump.

There were mountains of stuff there.

Old, ripped, wrecked, broken,

disgusting things.

Things that nobody wanted.

I did not want them, either.

"We are down in the dumps,"

I said to Sludge.

But then on top of one mountain

of junk I saw something!

A box was sticking out,

and I could see a big *R*

printed on one side of it!

At last! It must be Rosamond's box.

"We have to climb up that mountain

of junk," I said.

Sludge looked at me.

He did not want to do it.

I did not want to do it.

But we did it.

Up, up we climbed.

Over lumpy mattresses

and broken furniture

and old shoes and ugly clothes.

At last we were at the top of the heap.

I grabbed the empty box.

Now I could read the whole name on it.

RAT HOUSE.

It was not Rosamond's box.

It was a chewed-up box

that had once been a home

for Finley's rat.

I was mad.

I was tired.

Sludge was tired.

We sat down.

I put my arm around Sludge

and we sat there

on top of the world.

On top of the world of junk.

I looked down.

Down was *way* down.

I was afraid to stay

and afraid to leave.

But we had to leave.

"Let's go," I said.

Sludge and I started to climb down.

Sludge was scared.

"Don't look down," I said.

Sludge kept his eyes up.

Then I stopped.

That was it!

The answer to my case.

I had given myself the clue I needed!

"I have just solved the case," I said.

"We must go back to Rosamond's house."

I grabbed a lumpy mattress.

Sludge and I slid

the rest of the way down

on the mattress.

We brushed ourselves off.

Then we rushed to Rosamond's house.

She was sitting on the crate

with her cats, waiting for business.

"I delivered your note," she said.

"Did you find my box?"

"Yes," I said.

"So where is it?" she asked.

"You are sitting on it," I said.

"I'm sitting on a crate,

not a box," she said.

Rosamond and her cats stood up.

"See?"

I leaned down and picked up the crate.

And there, under it, was Rosamond's box!

"My box!" Rosamond said.

"It was inside my crate."

"Yes. Claude put the crate over the box,

but he didn't know it."

Rosamond picked up her box.

"Why didn't he know it?" she asked.

"Claude told me he was carrying
the crate near his stomach," I said,
"and he was looking for you
at the same time.

That meant he was looking
above the crate.

But what was happening *below*?

Claude did not know.

Claude did not look *down*.

Claude did not look down
when he put the crate over the box!

Then he started to run.

He fell. He kicked over the cans.

And that's when he noticed that
the box wasn't there.

After *he* had made it disappear."

"That's the last time I'll ask Claude
to help me," Rosamond said.

"Claude will be glad to hear that,"
I said.

Rosamond hugged her box.

"But how did you figure this out?"

"There were many clues," I said,

"but I didn't know it.

You told me that your box
was smaller than your crate.
That was a clue."

Rosamond was squeezing her box.

"Tell me more clues," she said.

"I saw crates in the supermarket,"
I said. "I figured you got your
BANANAS crate there."

"I bought lots and lots of bananas
at the supermarket," Rosamond said,
"until the banana crate was empty.
Then they gave it to me."

"I, Nate the Great, noticed that
all the crates at the supermarket
had an open top. That meant that
your crate must have an open top.
But you kept your crate upside down
to sit on.
The open top was at the bottom.
And it fit right over your box
and hid it."
Rosamond was all excited.
She was crushing her famous box.
I had done all my hard work
for a crushed box.
But my work was over.
I said, "I solved the case
when Sludge and I were at the dump

and I told him not to look down.

Not looking down was the key clue."

"You went to the dump for me!"

Rosamond exclaimed.

"I must do something for you.

I will read your future

two times for free. Three times.

Ten times. I will give you

as many futures

as you want."

"I can read my own future," I said.

I gazed into the crystal ball.

"I see a detective and his dog," I said.

"They are going to disappear."

And that's what Sludge and I did.

~Extra~ Fun Activities!

What's Inside

Nate's Notes: What's Down in the Dumps? 4

Nate's Notes: Unusual Pets 7

Nate's Notes: Pennies 13

Nate's Notes: Penny Campaigns 15

Make Your Own Money Box 16

Funny Pages 19

How to Make Puzzle Cupcakes 22

NATE'S NOTES:
What's Down in the Dumps?

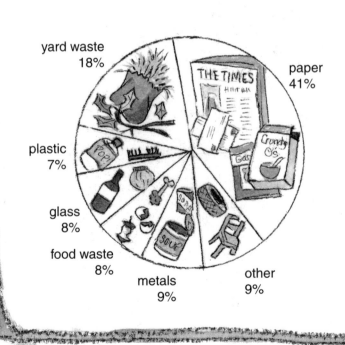

yard waste
18%

paper
41%

plastic
7%

glass
8%

food waste
8%

metals
9%

other
9%

More than half of what we throw away could be recycled!

YARD WASTE takes up lots of room in dumps. You can help solve this problem by starting a compost heap:

• Collect leaves and grass clippings.
• Pile them up in a corner of your yard or in a special recycling bin.

- Add natural material from the house—like used paper towels, coffee grounds, and eggshells.
- Wait about six months.
- (Optional) Add a few hundred worms.
- Finished compost looks like soil and smells earthy. Sprinkle it on your grass, flowers, trees, or shrubs to help keep them healthy!

EXTRA CREDIT: Bring home less paper, wrappings, and junk. You'll have less stuff to throw out!

NATE'S NOTES: Unusual Pets

Finley has a pet rat. Nate wanted to know: Was Finley weird? Nate went to the library. He found out that people have all kinds of pets—cats, dogs, and stranger creatures too.

American families own:

192 MILLION FISH. Aquarium fish are the most popular pets in America. That's good news because scientists say keeping fish is good for your health. Watching the fish swim calms you when you're stressed out. Some dentists even keep fish in their offices to relax their patients. And fish-keeping kids get better grades in school.

77.7 MILLION CATS. Cats are the second most popular kind of pets. Maybe that's because most cat owners have two or more. About nine out of ten cat owners say they talk to their cats. Cats may meow back—but they never meow at other cats. They save this sound just for their humans.

MEOW!
MEOW!

?

65 MILLION DOGS. Dog owners do silly things
too. They call home and leave messages
for the dog on the answering machine.
They sign the dog's name on greeting
cards. Many dog owners say they have
more photos of their dog than of their
husband or wife.

17.3 MILLION BIRDS. Birds are easy to keep in small spaces—making them good pets for city dwellers. They're also smart! Parrots, crows, mynah birds, and other feathered creatures can even learn to talk.

16.8 MILLION SMALL ANIMALS, including rats, mice, hamsters, gerbils, guinea pigs, ferrets, rabbits, potbellied pigs, and hedgehogs.

Hedgehogs? Okay, so Finley is <u>not</u> so weird.

8.8 MILLION REPTILES, like lizards, snakes, and turtles. These animals are getting popular, but they may not be the best pets for kids. Most reptiles don't like to be handled, and they need lots of care.

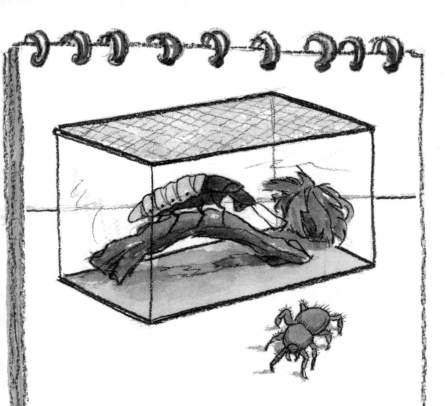

LOTS AND LOTS OF SPIDERS AND INSECTS,
such as tarantulas, hissing cockroaches,
scorpions, and ants. Pet owners who have
bugs are sometimes into the gross-out
factor. Sometimes they just like bugs.
Crickets are especially popular in Japan.
They're supposed to bring good luck.

NATE'S NOTES: Pennies

Rosamond's money box is big enough to hold a hundred dollars' worth of pennies. That's a lot of pennies. Nate learned more about pennies on the Web:

Pennies were the first money produced in the United States. A private mint made the first ones in 1787. The U.S. Mint took over the job in 1793. Over time, U.S. mints have pumped out more than 300 billion one-cent coins. Each one lasts about thirty years. The penny has had eleven different designs.

Today one side of a penny shows President Lincoln. He has been there since 1909, the year he would have turned 100. In 1959, the U.S. Mint added the Lincoln Memorial to the other side of the penny. That was to mark Lincoln's 150th birthday. If you inspect a penny, you will see the statue of Lincoln inside the memorial. That makes the penny the only coin that has the same person on both sides.

A mile of pennies laid out in a line with their sides touching amounts to $844.80. If you wanted to lay pennies from coast to coast, you'd need $2.5 million.

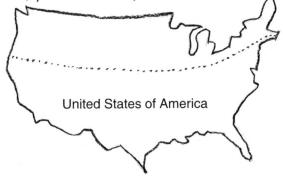

United States of America

NATE'S NOTES:
Penny Campaigns

Lots of charities collect pennies to do good work. Here are some that Nate found out about:

THE WORLD WILDLIFE FUND collects "Pennies for the Planet." They use the money to help big cats such as tigers and leopards survive in the wild.

ROOTS OF PEACE uses penny donations to create schools and playgrounds in war-torn countries like Angola in Africa and Afghanistan in Asia. Kids in the United States collect the pennies.

PASTA FOR PENNIES benefits the Leukemia and Lymphoma Society. Each year, more than a million students in 1,600 U.S. schools participate in this event. High earners win a pasta party for their class.

Make Your Own Money Box

*Rosamond has a special money box with her name on it.
You can make one too.*

Ask an adult to help you.

GET TOGETHER:

- an empty tissue box
- construction paper
- a pencil
- scissors
- glue
- old magazines

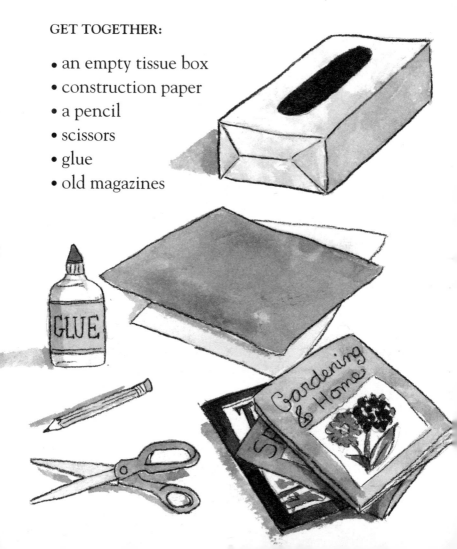

MAKE YOUR BOX:

1. Using the pencil, trace around each side of the box on the construction paper.
2. Cut out the pieces.
3. Glue each piece onto the matching side of the box. One piece will cover the hole in the top.
4. Have an adult use the scissors to cut around three sides of the box about an inch from the top. Bend back the cardboard on the attached side so that the box opens and closes.

5. Decorate your box! Use letters cut from a magazine to make a name collage. Or look for the letters to spell MONEY BOX, PRIVATE, or KEEP OUT.
6. Look in the magazines for other images related to money. You might find locks and keys, dollar signs, or piggy banks. Cut them out and glue them to your box.

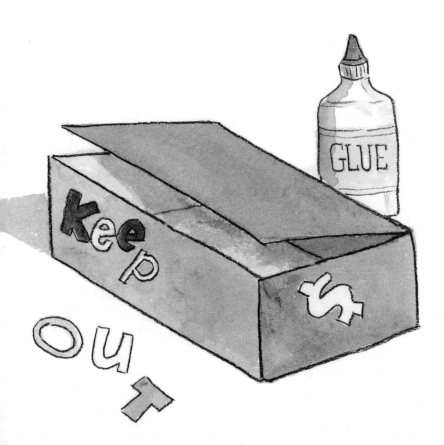

Funny Pages

Q: Where do fortune-tellers dance?
A: *At the crystal ball.*

Q: Where did the
fortune-teller go
on her vacation?
A: *Palm Beach.*

Q: What do you call a short fortune-teller
who escapes from prison?
A: *A small medium at large!*

Q: What has a head and a tail but no body?
A: *A penny!*

Q: Where can you get change in the forest?
A: *A skunk usually has some scents.*

Q: What do you give your money when it's sick?
A: *Penny-cillin.*

How to Make Puzzle Cupcakes

Nate likes solving mysteries. He also likes puzzle cupcakes.

You need an oven to bake the cupcakes.
Ask an adult to help you with this recipe.

Makes eighteen cupcakes.

GET TOGETHER:

- one package of cake mix (any flavor)
- the ingredients listed on the box (usually you'll need water, oil, and eggs)
- a mixing bowl
- an electric mixer
- a large cake pan (9 inches by 13 inches)
- 18 paper cupcake cups
- 2 tablespoons powdered sugar
- a flour sifter

MAKE YOUR CUPCAKES:

1. Preheat the oven to 350 degrees.
2. Prepare the cake mix. Look on the box for the directions.
3. Put the cupcake cups in the pan.
4. Fill each cup about halfway.
5. Bake 30 minutes.

6. Cool completely. Your cupcakes should be funny shapes—like the pieces of a jigsaw puzzle.
7. Put the powdered sugar in the sifter. Sift the sugar over the cupcakes.
8. Separate the cupcakes. Try to put the puzzle back together.
9. Give up and eat!

Have you helped solve all Nate the Great's mysteries?

❏ **Nate the Great**: Meet Nate, the great detective, and join him as he uses incredible sleuthing skills to solve his first big case.

❏ **Nate the Great Goes Undercover**: Who— or what—is raiding Oliver's trash every night? Nate bravely hides out in his friend's garbage can to catch the smelly crook.

❏ **Nate the Great and the Lost List**: Nate loves pancakes, but who ever heard of cats eating them? Is a strange recipe at the heart of this mystery?

❏ **Nate the Great and the Phony Clue**: Against ferocious cats, hostile adversaries, and a sly phony clue, Nate struggles to prove that he's still the world's greatest detective.

❏ **Nate the Great and the Sticky Case**: Nate is stuck with his stickiest case yet as he hunts for his friend Claude's valuable stegosaurus stamp.

❏ **Nate the Great and the Missing Key**: Nate isn't afraid to look anywhere—even under the nose of his friend's ferocious dog, Fang—to solve the case of the missing key.

❑ **Nate the Great and the Snowy Trail**: Nate has his work cut out for him when his friend Rosamond loses the birthday present she was going to give him. How can he find the present when Rosamond won't even tell him what it is?

❑ **Nate the Great and the Fishy Prize**: The trophy for the Smartest Pet Contest has disappeared! Will Sludge, Nate's clue-sniffing dog, help solve the case and prove he's worthy of the prize?

❑ **Nate the Great Stalks Stupidweed**: When his friend Oliver loses his special plant, Nate searches high and low. Who knew a little weed could be so tricky?

❑ **Nate the Great and the Boring Beach Bag**: It's no relaxing day at the beach for Nate and his trusty dog, Sludge, as they search through sand and surf for signs of a missing beach bag.

❑ **Nate the Great Goes Down in the Dumps**: Nate discovers that the only way to clean up this case is to visit the town dump. Detective work can sure get dirty!

❑ **Nate the Great and the Halloween Hunt**: It's Halloween, but Nate isn't trick-or-treating for candy. Can any of the witches, pirates, and robots he meets help him find a missing cat?

❑ **Nate the Great and the Musical Note**: Nate is used to looking for clues, not listening for them! When he gets caught in the middle of a musical riddle, can he hear his way out?

❑ **Nate the Great and the Stolen Base**: It's not easy to track down a stolen base, and Nate's hunt leads him to some strange places before he finds himself at bat once more.

❑ **Nate the Great and the Pillowcase**: When a pillowcase goes missing, Nate must venture into the dead of night to search for clues. Everyone sleeps easier knowing Nate the Great is on the case!

❑ **Nate the Great and the Mushy Valentine**: Nate hates mushy stuff. But when someone leaves a big heart taped to Sludge's doghouse, Nate must help his favorite pooch discover his secret admirer.

❑ **Nate the Great and the Tardy Tortoise**: Where did the mysterious green tortoise in Nate's yard come from? Nate needs all his patience to follow this slow . . . slow . . . clue.

❑ **Nate the Great and the Crunchy Christmas**: It's Christmas, and Fang, Annie's scary dog, is not feeling jolly. Can Nate find Fang's crunchy Christmas mail before Fang crunches on *him*?

❑ **Nate the Great Saves the King of Sweden**: Can Nate solve his *first-ever* international case without leaving his own neighborhood?

❑ **Nate the Great and Me: The Case of the Fleeing Fang**: A surprise Happy Detective Day party is great fun for Nate until his friend's dog disappears! Help Nate track down the missing pooch, and learn all the tricks of the trade in a special fun section for aspiring detectives.

❑ **Nate the Great and the Monster Mess**: Nate loves his mother's deliciously spooky Monster Cookies, but the recipe has vanished! This is one case Nate and his growling stomach can't afford to lose.

❑ **Nate the Great, San Francisco Detective**: Nate visits his cousin Olivia Sharp in the big city, but it's no vacation. Can he find a lost joke book in time to save the world?

❑ **Nate the Great and the Big Sniff**: Nate depends on his dog, Sludge, to help him solve all his cases. But Nate is on his own this time, because Sludge has disappeared! Can Nate solve the case and recover his canine buddy?

❑ **Nate the Great on the Owl Express**: Nate boards a train to guard Hoot, his cousin Olivia Sharp's pet owl. Then Hoot vanishes! Can Nate find out *whooo* took the feathered creature?